Thomas and the Hurricane

Christopher Awdry

Illustrated by Stephen Lings

HEINEMANN: LONDON

William Heinemann Ltd
Michelin House
81 Fulham Road
London SW3 6RB

LONDON MELBOURNE AUCKLAND

Copyright © William Heinemann Ltd 1992
ISBN 0 434 96133 7
Produced by Mandarin Offset
Printed in China.

A hurricane force wind was sweeping across the Island of Sodor.
Thomas, Percy and Toby listened anxiously as it howled around
their shed.

It rattled the windows and moaned in the roof.
It was even strong enough to shake the heavy wooden doors.

Thomas, Percy and Toby did not get very much sleep that night.
When their drivers came the next morning none of the engines
wanted to go out.

"It's much nicer in here," said Percy. "Warm," added Toby.
"I know a Railway where the trains don't run on very windy days,"
said Thomas hopefully.

His driver laughed. "So do I," he said, "but we're not it. Come on – what would the Fat Controller do without us?"

"Brrr!" shivered Thomas.
The wind was cold as well as strong, and Annie and Clarabel didn't like it either.

There weren't many passengers that morning.
They all wanted to stay indoors and Thomas didn't blame them.
"Lucky things," he thought.

But when Thomas reached the station by the river he was astonished to see footballers playing in the nearby field, one team wearing red shirts, the other in blue and white.

"It's part of the Knockout Competition," explained the fireman.
"At the end of the season the winners will get a silver cup."

Trees between field and railway waved wildly in the wind.
"Sooner them than me," Thomas muttered to himself.
"They'll all get knocked out if they're not careful."

James was waiting at the Junction. He didn't mind the wind, he said, and was even boasting about it. "My train was dead on time," he announced proudly. "A little bit of wind can't stop me."

Just then the wind blew so hard that the station roof shook, and so did
something else.
"Just look at that signal!" exclaimed Thomas.

But James couldn't see, because suddenly the signal wasn't there any more. The wind had blown it down.

"Help!" said Thomas in alarm, as two more signal posts broke and crashed to the ground. "Let's get away from here."

The fireman hurried to the signal-box to find out what they should do.
"We can't move without signals," explained the driver.
"How do we know if it's safe?"

"Well, it's not safe here either," snorted James.
The drivers laughed, but they did move the engines along the platform
as far as they dared.

It was lucky that they did, because two minutes later the wind lifted the platform canopy clean off its framework and dropped it, to shatter on the platform below.

No one was hurt as the canopy crashed down, but Annie and Clarabel were very badly frightened, and some splinters of wood scratched Clarabel's paint.

At last a man with flags came and signalled the two trains away.
James wasn't boasting about being dead on time any more.
He was only too glad to get away.

Thomas reached the station by the river and stopped for a drink.
The fireman had a job to put the pipe in Thomas's tank,
because the wind kept trying to blow it away.

They were ready at last. "Come along, and let's get home.
Oh come along and let's get home," Thomas puffed to Annie and Clarabel.
They came as quickly as they could.

By the time they reached the curve near the football ground
they were going well.
The footballers were still playing. Thomas was amazed.

They were halfway round the curve when suddenly there was a jerk,
and the guard's emergency brake went hard on.
"Oooooer," groaned Thomas. "What's the matter now?"

He soon found out. Suddenly, lying across the line in front of him he saw an enormous tree, where the wind had left it.

Thomas stopped just in time. "Good gracious!" he exclaimed.
"I couldn't see that, so how did the guard know about it?"

His driver looked back. Running towards them, waving their red jerseys, were three footballers, followed by the guard, who was waving a red flag and blowing his whistle.

"Thank goodness you stopped," panted the footballers when they arrived. "We thought we were too late."

"It was a near thing," said the driver. "Thank you for warning us."

The driver took Thomas back to the station by the river, and
Bertie came for his passengers. Thomas had to spend a cold night there
because he could go no further until the line was clear.

The next day Terence the tractor came and dragged the tree off the line.
It was cut up into small pieces. Toby and Percy worked hard all day
taking the wood away, and at last Thomas, Annie and Clarabel could go home.

A week later there was a party at the station by the river. All the engines were there and the Fat Controller gave the footballers a framed certificate to remind them of the day they saved the train.